Adventure at Hogwarts™
D1252411

Untangle the lines from each founder of Hogwarts to the crest that represents their house.

Count all the wands below and write the number in the frame.
Draw a line to match this Dementor to its correct shape.
1
2
3
4
5

Draw a line to lead Harry to his friends by moving only along spaces with the Gryffindor crest.

GRYFFINDOR

START

		GRYFFINDOR	HUFFLEPUFF	GRYFFINDOR	GRYFFINDOR	HUFFLEPUFF
		HUFFLEPUFF	GRYFFINDOR	SLYTHERIN	RAVENCLAW	GRYFFINDOR
RAVENCLAW	GRYFFINDOR	SLYTHERIN	GRYFFINDOR	RAVENCLAW	GRYFFINDOR	SLYTHERIN
GRYFFINDOR	SLYTHERIN	GRYFFINDOR	HUFFLEPUFF	RAVENCLAW	SLYTHERIN	GRYFFINDOR
HUFFLEPUFF	RAVENCLAW	SLYTHERIN	RAVENCLAW	GRYFFINDOR	GRYFFINDOR	SLYTHERIN
RAVENCLAW	GRYFFINDOR	GRYFFINDOR	GRYFFINDOR	HUFFLEPUFF		
GRYFFINDOR	SLYTHERIN	RAVENCLAW	SLYTHERIN			
HUFFLEPUFF	GRYFFINDOR	GRYFFINDOR	GRYFFINDOR			

FINISH

Look at the scene below. Draw lines to match the missing puzzle pieces to their correct places.

The Forbidden Forest is a dangerous place that students should keep away from. Connect the dots to complete the picture of Aragog!
What's hairy and has four legs? Me and Harry running away as fast as we can!

A big cluster of spiders lives in the Forbidden Forest but only two spiders are identical. Find and circle them.

Match Harry, Ron, and Hermione to their words. Then untangle the lines to see where each is hiding. Write the correct number in the circles.
1
2
3
Expecto Patronum!
I'm going to bed before either of you come up with another clever idea to get us killed. Or worse, expelled!
Sunshine, daisies, butter mellow, turn this stupid, fat rat yellow!

Draw an expression on Hermione's face according to the description.

1

After arguing with Draco

2

After Gryffindor won the House Cup

3

After she saw the troll in the girls' bathroom

This is Hogsmeade, a magical village near Hogwarts. Look at it closely and check off which statements are true and which are false.

T F

There is only one snowman.

Hermione's cat is running in the snow.

Harry is arranging Christmas ornaments.

Professor McGonagall is holding an umbrella.

To conjure a Patronus, a magical spirit protector, a witch or wizard must think of their happiest memory. What's your happiest memory? Draw it below!

Which picture piece can't be matched to this illustration? Circle it!

The Basilisk is a giant serpent with a deadly stare. Help Harry get away from the creature by leading him through the pipes to Fawkes.

Harry used the legendary Sword of Gryffindor to fight the Basilisk. Circle the real weapon among its copies.

Ron is thinking about a certain animal. It appears in his thought bubble only once. Circle it!

Complete the grid of Quidditch equipment by filling in the numbers so that each row and column has four different things.

Mr. Filch, the caretaker of Hogwarts, loves his cat, Mrs. Norris. Color in the shapes with the designated color to see what she looks like.

Read the character names and descriptions below. Then write the letter of the character name that matches his or her description.

A Ron Weasley

B Hermione Granger

C Professor Dumbledore

D Professor McGonagall

Long-bearded headmaster of Hogwarts

Transfiguration professor who wears a pointed hat

Gryffindor student who is afraid of spiders

Gryffindor student who receives top marks

Which hat is identical to the one
Professor McGonagall is wearing? Circle it!
1
2
3
4
5
Which Hogwarts house would you like to belong to?
Color the scarf with its colors!

Platform 9 ¾ is a magical place from which the Hogwarts Express departs. Draw a line to follow the arrows and help Harry catch the train!

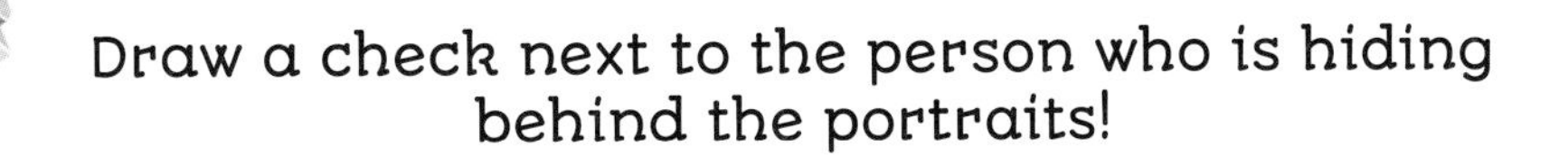

Draw a check next to the person who is hiding behind the portraits!

Look at the wand movements Hermione makes while practicing the Levitation spell and complete the sequences.

Scabbers has jumped on Hagrid's shoulder.
Complete the maze to help him get down.
Gulping gargoyles, it tickles!
START
FINISH

Harry and Ron are in a hurry to get to Hogwarts. Find the picture pieces below and write down their coordinates.

One of the Dementors is different from the rest.
Find and circle it.
1
2
3
4
5
6
7
8
Find and circle the names of the characters
hidden in the grid below.
DUMBLEDORE
HARRY
HERMIONE
RON
B D R A N B S R O N B A D F R
B U H C V C D P Y N S A D F T
A M C C A W T C U B T U O Z F
N B B L E D O R E H E R M U O
R L M D U M B L E H A R R Y A
H E V C B J P U I S V A R B X
A D C C A W T C Q B T U O Z F
B O H C V H E R M I O N E F T
B R R A N B S R A N B A D F R
N E B L E D O R E H E R M I O

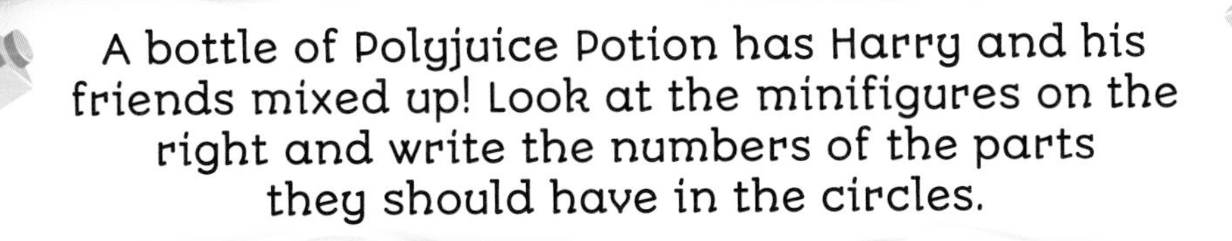

A bottle of Polyjuice Potion has Harry and his friends mixed up! Look at the minifigures on the right and write the numbers of the parts they should have in the circles.

Ron

1

2

3

Harry

4

5

6

Hermione

7

8

9

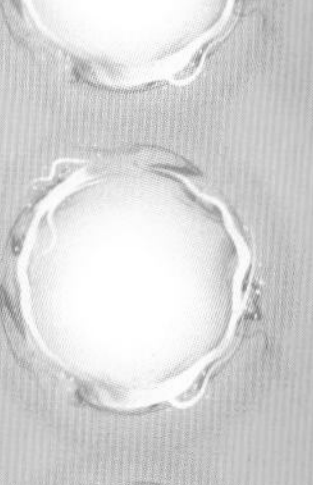

Hogwarts is a magical school, unlike any other! Look at the picture and write the answers to the questions below.

In which square can you see a flying car?

How many Dementors are there in the picture?

How many towers are there in square C2?

In how many squares can you see dragons?

In how many squares can you see boats?

Which set of robes is the same as the one Hermione is wearing? Circle it!
1
2
3
4
5
Ron first uses the Levitation spell correctly when he, Hermione, and Harry battle a troll. Draw the troll here!

Use the key below to find and color in Ron's,
Ginny's, and Hermione's Paronuses.

Cedric Diggory, along with Harry, represented Hogwarts in the Triwizard Tournament. Which of the picture pieces doesn't match Cedric's photo? Circle it!

Write the number of each picture piece in the empty spaces to create the Gryffindor crest.

Harry's photo appears often in *The Daily Prophet*, a popular wizarding newspaper. Follow the instructions to draw Harry's portrait step by step.

Christmas at Hogwarts is magical!
Fill in this festive scene by drawing a line to match the puzzle pieces to the empty spaces.

Draw a line to connect the characters
with their Patronuses.
Hint: Look at the color combinations
in the boxes next to them.

Use a mirror to read the words. Then draw a line to match the words with their pictures.

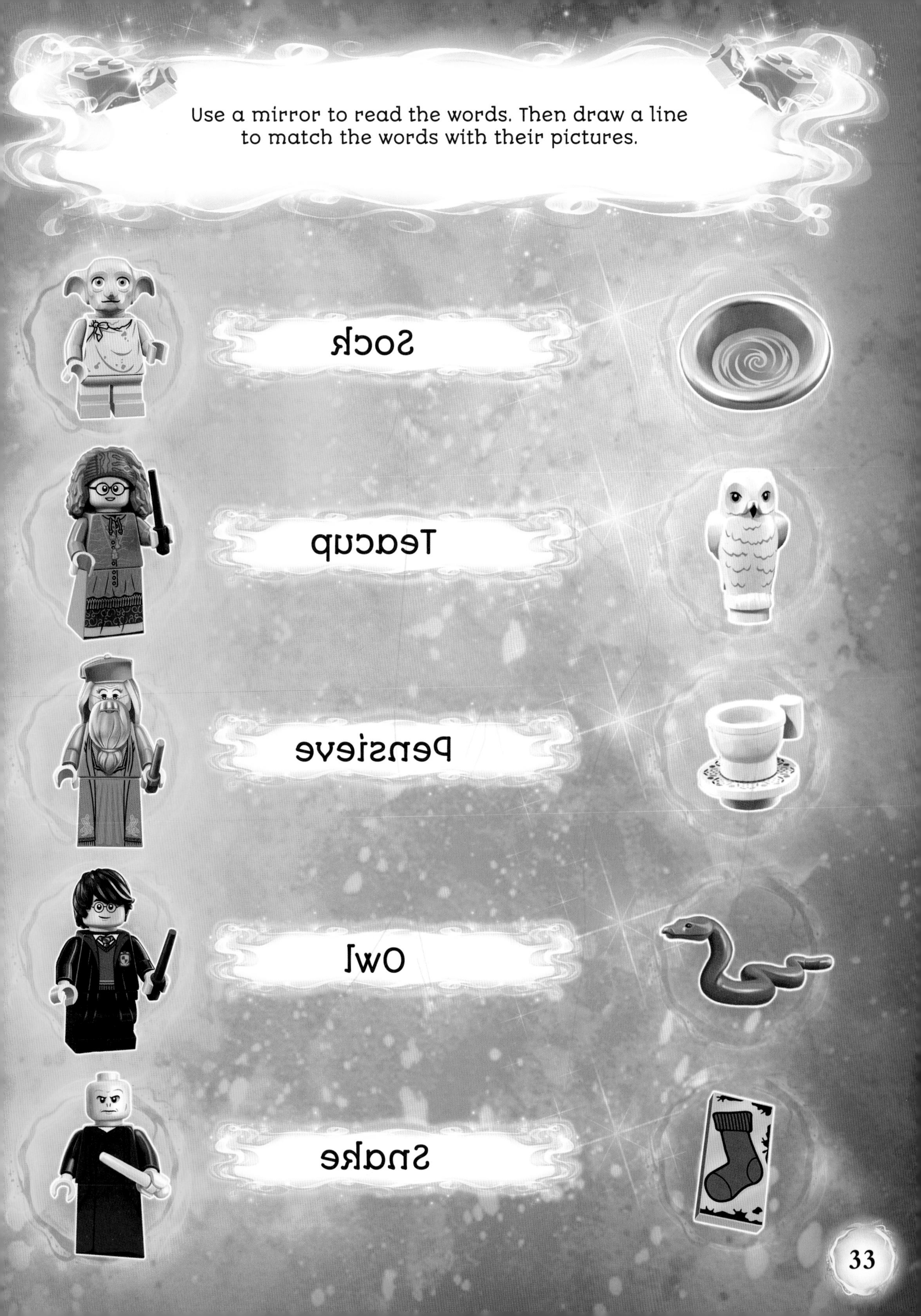

Dementors are scary. Draw them funny faces so that they don't look creepy anymore!

Find and circle five differences on
Ron's photo on the right.

Read the hints and circle the professor Harry
is looking for.

He's not a woman. He doesn't
wear a turban. He doesn't
wear glasses but has a beard.

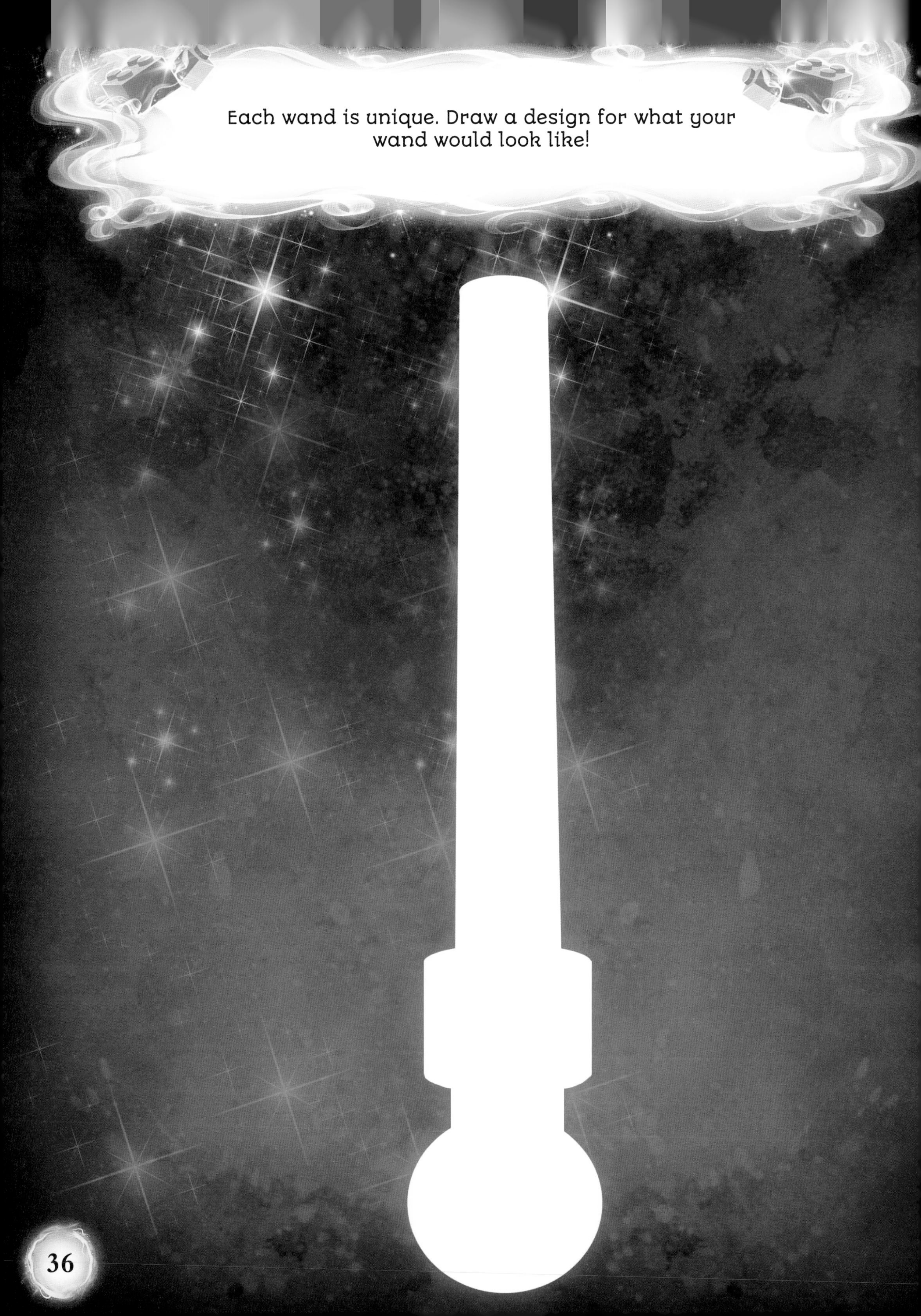
Each wand is unique. Draw a design for what your wand would look like!

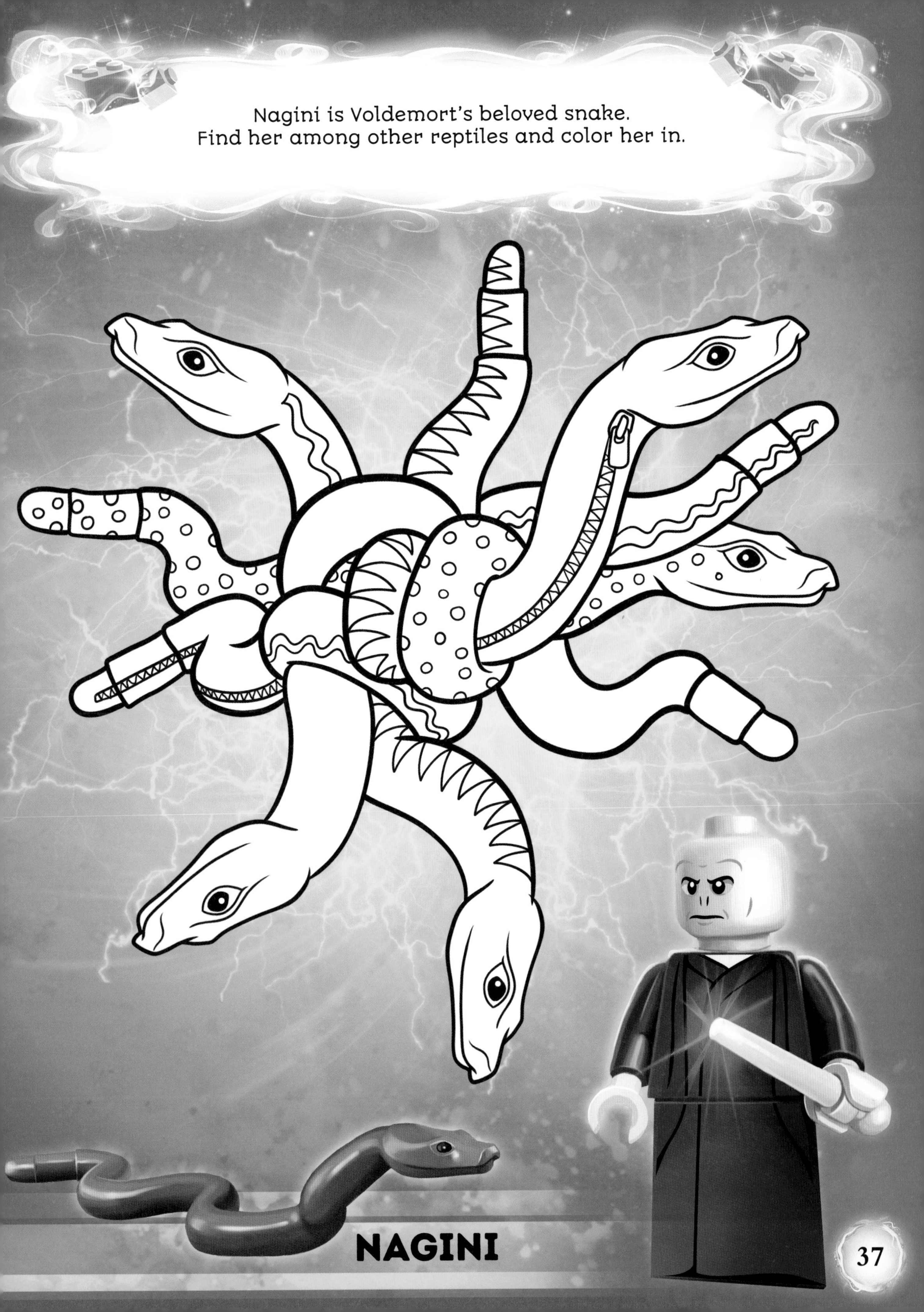
Nagini is Voldemort's beloved snake.
Find her among other reptiles and color her in.
NAGINI

The Mirror of Erised shows the reflected person's deepest desire. Draw a line to match the missing fragments to each of the reflections.

A Boggart is a magical creature that takes the shape of whatever the person facing it fears most. Untangle the lines to reveal each person's fear. Then write the number in the circles below.
1
2
3

When Polyjuice Potion begins to wear off,
the true form of the drinker begins to show.
Find the real Harry by writing the number of the
person who took his form from the characters below.

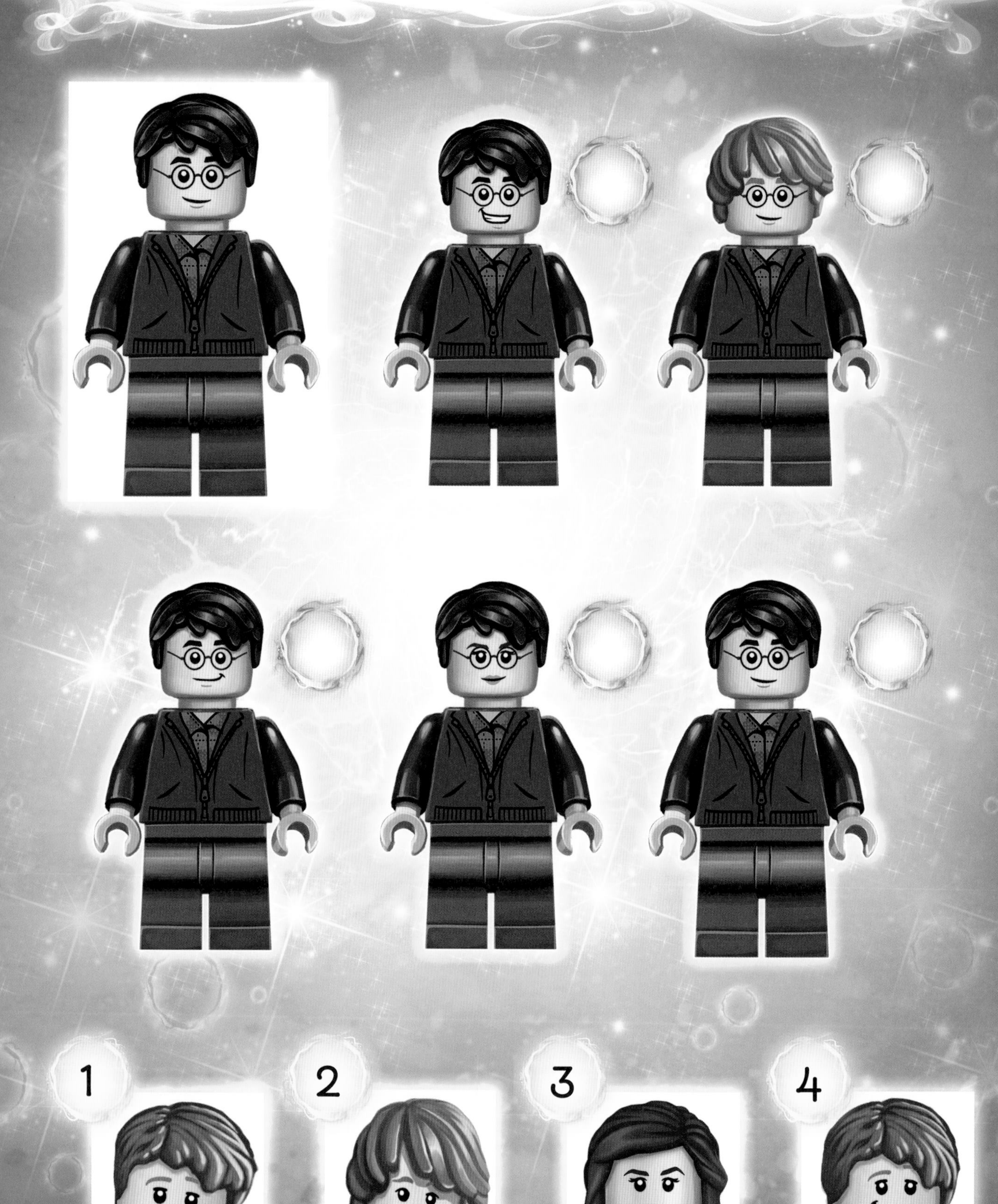

Brooms are a very important piece of Quidditch equipment. Draw a picture of Harry catching the Golden Snitch on his broomstick below.

Potions classes are held in the Hogwarts dungeons. In each set of picture pieces below, mark the one that corresponds to the dungeons.

Hermione Granger is a a smart and loyal witch.
Follow the instructions to draw her.

In each row, circle one character who doesn't belong.
1
2
3
4

Can you find two identical faces Harry Potter is making? Circle them!

How many brooms can you see in this picture?
Write your answer in the frame!
Mr. Ollivander makes wands with unicorn hair cores, dragon heartstring cores, and phoenix feather cores. Draw a unicorn, dragon, and phoenix below!

These are the banners for the four Hogwarts houses. There's a small mistake on each of their mirror images. Find and circle them all!

Test your magical knowledge! Match the characters with their descriptions by writing the correct numbers in the circles.

1 Potions master at Hogwarts

2 Not many people like to say his name

3 Harry's half-giant friend

4 Blond Slytherin student

5 Harry's friend who is very smart

6 Harry's freckle-faced friend

7 Professor with a white beard

8 Head of Gryffindor house

9 A wizard who owns a snowy owl

Harry is fighting his final battle with Voldemort at Hogwarts! Lead the beam from Harry's wand to the Dark Lord, moving only along the red circles.

Connect the dots to complete the image of the Quidditch Cup.

Dobby, the free house-elf, is hiding somewhere among the socks. Find and circle him.

All the professors gather in the Great Hall for the start-of-term banquet. Write the number of the missing professor in the empty spaces.

When the Death Eaters took over the Ministry of Magic, a wanted poster was issued for Harry! Draw Harry's face in it below.

UNDESIRABLE
№ 1

HARRY POTTER

Professor Slughorn is thinking about a combination of ingredients to help Harry win the Felix Felicis potion, also called "Liquid Luck." Use his key to circle the ingredients in the grid below.

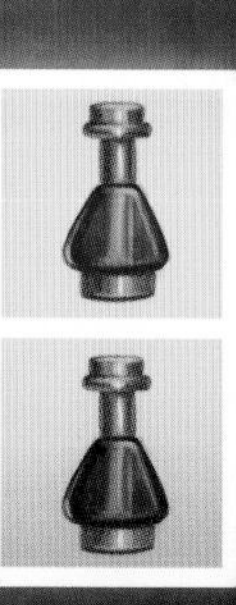

In the first task of the Triwizard Tournament,
Harry had to face the Hungarian Horntail.
Which of the shapes belongs to this dragon?
Circle the letter!
A
B
C
D
E

Hogwarts professors are very unusual people.
One of them sometimes even turns into a werewolf!
It's the professor who appears only once in this grid.
Find and circle that professor!

All the professors are here!
What a nightmare . . .

Ron Weasley is Harry Potter's best friend.
Learn how to draw him by following
the step-by-step instructions.

Harry Potter's world is full of magical objects. Find two identical elements in the boxes connected with arrows and circle them.

Match the animal to its Hogwarts house crest by writing its number in the correct spaces.
RAVENCLAW
SLYTHERIN
HUFFLEPUFF
GRYFFINDOR
1
2
3
4
Harry, Ron, and Hermione need all the following items for their first year at Hogwarts. Write the number of the items they still need in the circles below.
1
2
3
4
5
6
7

Answers

p. 4

4  1

3  2

p. 5

13

2

p. 6

p. 7

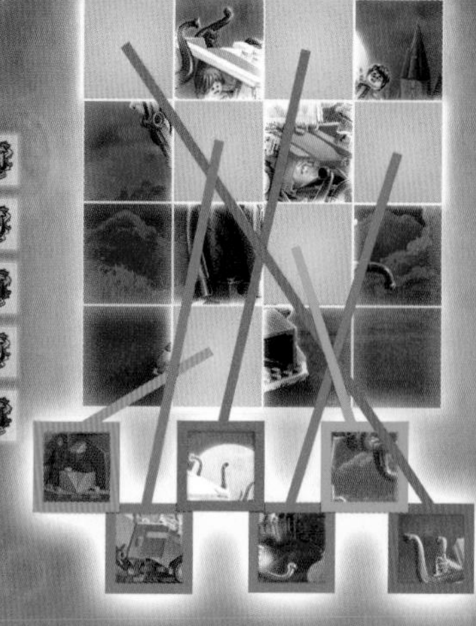

p. 8

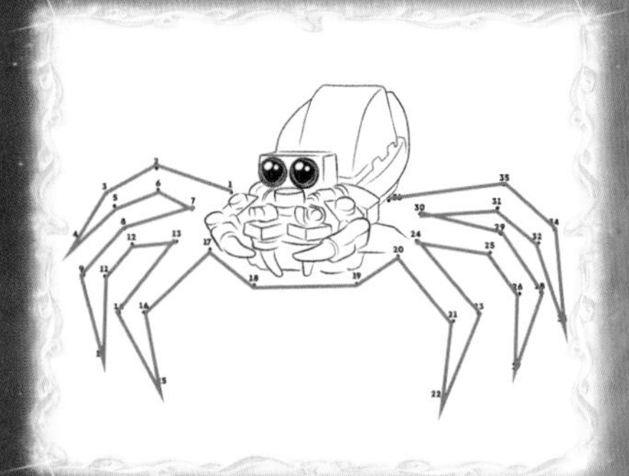

p. 9

p. 10

p. 12

T	F
✓	
	✓
	✓
	✓

p. 14

p. 15

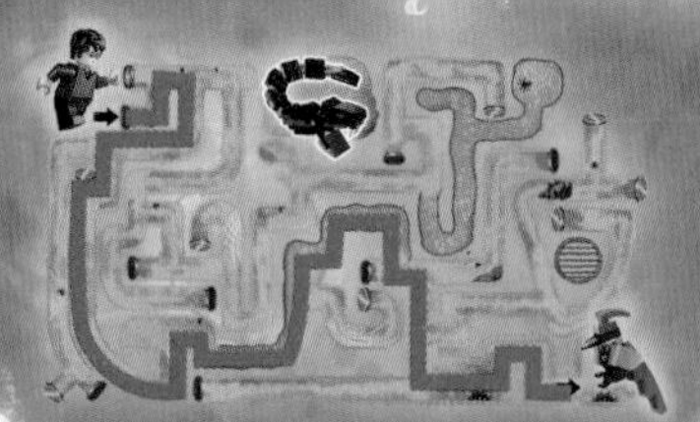

p. 16

4	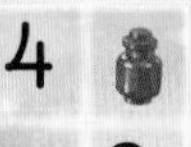		3
	2	1	4
2	4	3	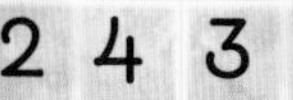
1			2

p. 17

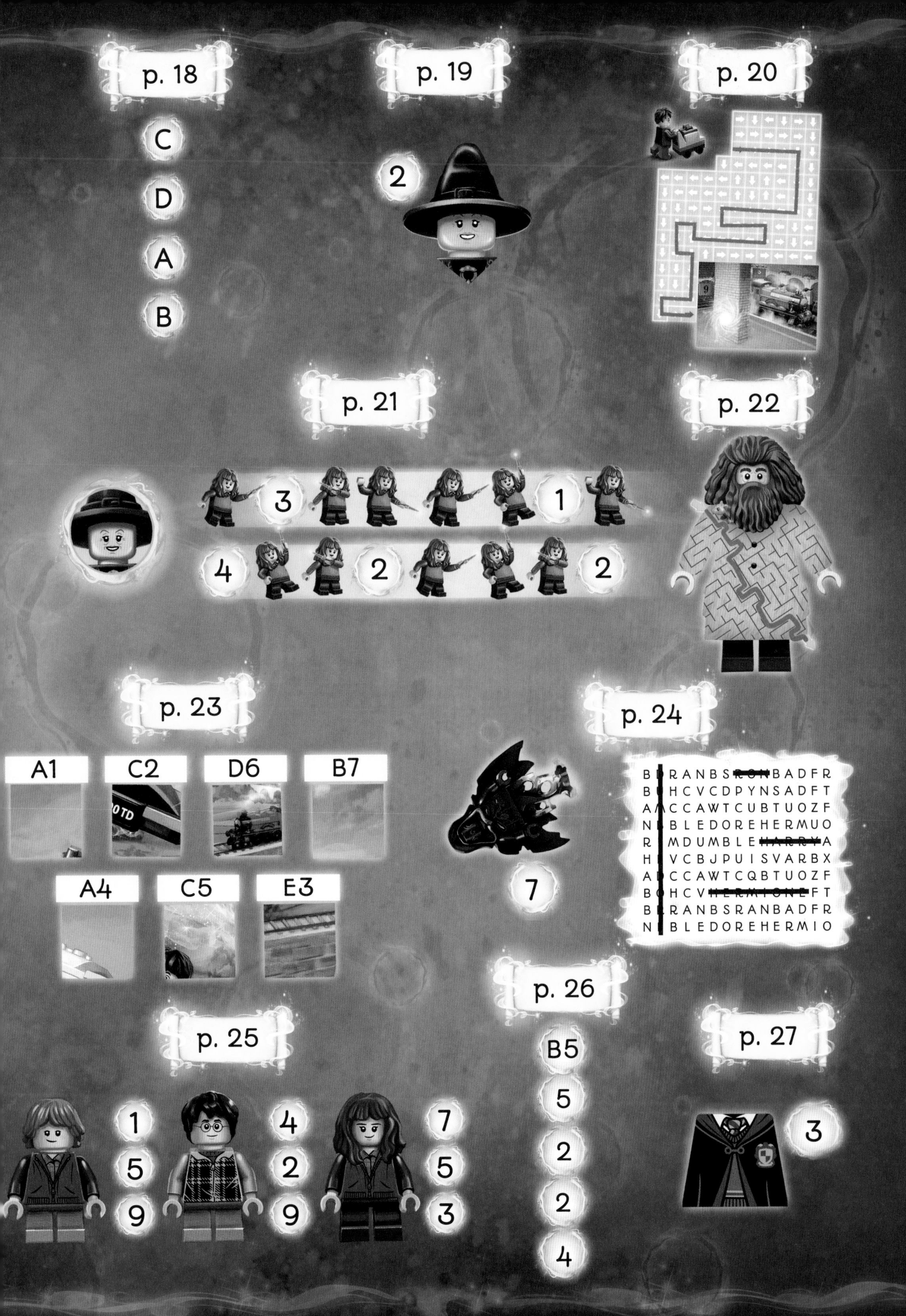

p. 18
C
D
A
B
p. 19
2
p. 20
9
p. 21
3
1
4
2
2
p. 22
p. 23
A1
C2
D6
B7
A4
C5
E3
p. 24
7
B D R A N B S R O N B A D F R
B U H C V C D P Y N S A D F T
A M C C A W T C U B T U O Z F
N B B L E D O R E H E R M U O
R L M D U M B L E H A R R Y A
H E V C B J P U I S V A R B X
A D C C A W T C Q B T U O Z F
B O H C V H E R M I O N E F T
B R R A N B S R A N B A D F R
N E B L E D O R E H E R M I O
p. 25
1
5
9
4
2
9
7
5
3
p. 26
B5
5
2
2
4
p. 27
3

p. 28
p. 29
5
1
2
4
3
p. 31
p. 32
p. 33
3
5
1
p. 35
p. 37
p. 38
4
3
1
2
p. 39
2
3
1
p. 40
4
2
1
3
p. 42
A
A
B

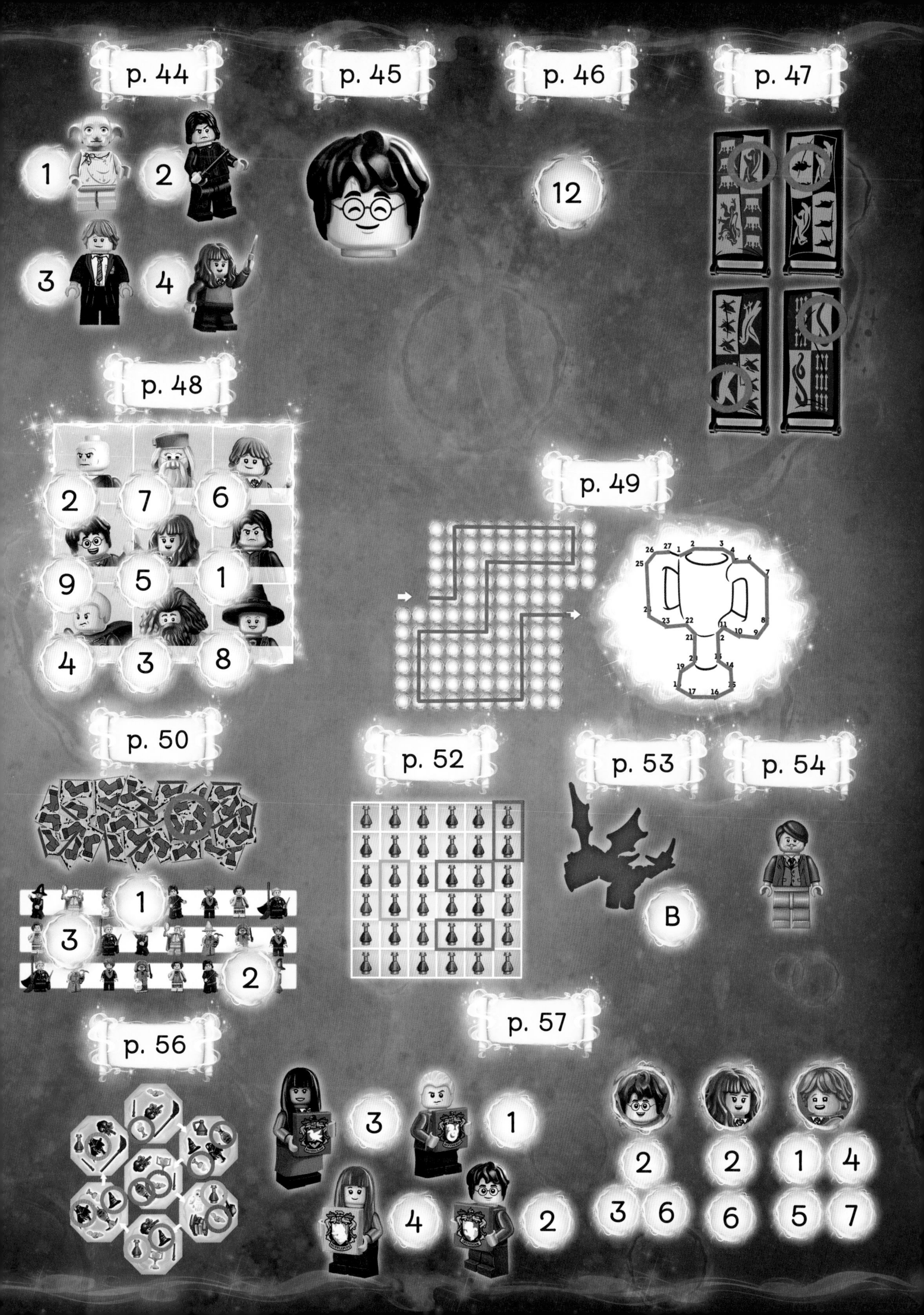
p. 44
1
2
3
4
p. 45
p. 46
12
p. 47
p. 48
2
7
6
9
5
1
4
3
8
p. 49
p. 50
1
3
2
p. 52
p. 53
B
p. 54
p. 56
p. 57
3
1
4
2
2
2
1
4
3
6
6
5
7

How to build Ron Weasley